Enid Blyton's™

ENCHANTED LANDS

The Magic OF THE Faraway Tree

Hippo

Deep in the middle of the Enchanted Wood grows a most extraordinary tree - the Magic Faraway Tree. Some of its branches are like those of an oak tree, and others like beech or birch. Most extraordinary of all, the tree bears fruits of all different kinds - apples and peaches, plums and cherries, walnuts and pine cones. The tree is so tall that its branches reach high into the clouds, and on the topmost branch is a ladder. If you climb up the ladder into the clouds, you will find yourself in one of the strange enchanted lands that come to rest at the top of the tree.

The tree is home to Moonface, Saucepan Man, Silky the fairy, Dame Washalot, the Angry Pixie and Mr Watzisname, as well as birds and animals. The folk of the Faraway Tree have many visitors, among them three children, Joe, Fran and Beth. The children live in a cottage on the edge of the Enchanted Wood and whenever they can, they climb up the tree to see Moonface, Saucepan Man and Silky and sometimes they climb up the ladder, through the hole in the clouds, to visit the lands at the top of the tree . . .

The Magic
OF THE
Faraway Tree

8·3·00

To my not so little
Gwendolyn

Lots of love
Auntie
Ceara
:)

xo xo

Scholastic Children's Books
Commonwealth House
1-19 New Oxford Street
London WC1A 1NU, UK
a division of Scholastic Ltd
London * New York * Toronto * Sydney * Auckland

First published in 1997 by Hippo, an imprint of Scholastic Ltd

Copyright in original stories and characters Enid Blyton Ltd *Enid Blyton*™
Audio-visual series copyright Abbey Home Entertainment Limited 1997
Story consultant Gillian Baverstock
All rights reserved

ISBN 0 590 11169 8

2 4 6 8 10 9 7 5 3 1

Printed by Proost, Belgium

The Land of Toys

One beautiful morning, Joe, Fran and Beth were climbing up through the branches of the Faraway Tree. Joe called down to the others.

"Come on! Honestly! Any slower and you'll be going backwards!"

"Sorry?" called a voice from above. Joe looked up to see Beth grinning down at him.

"Er . . . nothing," he muttered. "Hurry up, Fran!"

Further down the tree, Fran was just passing Silky's house when Silky flew out of her window.

"Whoops! Sorry, Fran. Have you come for Saucepan Man's party?"

"Party? Ooh, I love parties!" cried Fran. "All the ice-cream and balloons and games - will there be games? Statues is my favourite! I'm really good at musical statues. I can stand as still as a . . . as a . . . I can stand as still as a tiger! I adore sausages on sticks and . . ."

Fran carried on chattering as she and Silky caught up with Joe and Beth.

"Why is Saucepan having a party? Is it his birthday? He must be terribly old. We should have brought him a present but we haven't, because we didn't know. Will he mind, do you think? What . . ."

"FRAN!" cried Silky, as she tried to get a word in. "No, it's not his birthday. He doesn't *have* a birthday. He just has a party in Moonface's house every time the Land of Goodies arrives at the top of the Faraway Tree."

"The Land of Goodies? What's that?" asked Beth as the children followed Silky into Moonface's house.

Silky began to unload her basket. "It's a wonderful place where sweets and cakes and biscuits just grow on trees. You can pick as many as you like, and it's all free!"

Joe looked at the sweets that Silky was putting on the table. "I thought you said Saucepan Man was bringing all the goodies."

"He is," said Silky, smiling. "I just had a few things left over from the last party. These are Google Buns, and that's a Pop Biscuit."

"What's this?" asked Joe, picking up an odd-looking sweet.

"That? That's a Toffee Shock," said Silky.

Joe popped the sweet into his mouth. "It would take a pretty special toffee to shock me," he boasted. A few seconds later, Joe could hardly speak. The toffee in his mouth was growing larger and larger. His cheeks bulged out until he thought they would burst. Sparks crackled round him, then he was lifted off his feet and whirled around the room like a giant sparkler.

Suddenly, there was a loud explosion inside Joe's mouth and the toffee completely disappeared. Joe sat down on the floor with a bump, a surprised look on his face. "Wow! That was a *very* special toffee!" he said.

From outside they heard a fierce voice shouting, "Keep the noise down in there!" The door opened and Moonface backed into the room, followed by the Angry Pixie, still shouting.

"You ought to be ashamed of yourself! How's a pixie supposed to get any sleep with that row going on!"

"Yes, yes. I'm very sorry," said Moonface. "I didn't realise I was being so noisy."

The Angry Pixie walked out of Moonface's house, slamming the door behind him.

"Silly old buffoon!" muttered Moonface, then jumped as he noticed the group standing behind him. "Aha! Visitors!" He looked round his room and noticed all the party food and the balloons and streamers. "What's going on? Is there a party?"

"Yes!" cried Fran. "It's Saucepan Man's party! He's having it in your house. Silky said that he's gone to the Land of Goodies to get all the party food and . . ."

Moonface slapped his head. "Oh no! The Land of Goodies?"

"Is something the matter, Moonface?" asked Beth.

"I'll say there is," he replied. "The Land of Goodies won't be at the top of the tree for another week!"

The children looked worried. "Where do you think he is, then?" asked Joe.

Moonface turned towards the door. "We'd better go and find out," he said.

The three children and Silky followed Moonface out of the door and up the tree to the ladder. One by one they climbed through the cloud to see what land was floating there . . .

"Wow! . . ." cried Joe as he and the others looked around them. "Wow!"

They were in the Land of Toys. Everywhere they looked were toys. All the toys that had ever been invented were there and each one was alive. Kites were swooping past, the sky was full of toy rockets and aeroplanes and helicopters. Toy cars sped along the roads and little trains ran along railway lines. A skateboard rolled up to Beth and said cheekily, "Hiya Toots! Want a ride?"

"You can talk!" cried Beth in amazement.

"So can you!" laughed the skateboard. "Hop on!"

Beth jumped onto the skateboard which zoomed off. Silky flew after them calling, "Race you there and back again!"

In another part of the Land of Toys stood a toy fort. At the entrance to the fort, two soldiers grasped Saucepan Man by each arm. He was struggling to get free and was so angry and

frightened that he got his words muddled up.

"Let me go! This is an outbreak . . . an outright . . . an outrage! I haven't done anything!"

"You call pinching a load of sweets nothing?" snapped one of the soldiers.

"What?" cried Saucepan Man. "But I . . ."

"Where do you think you are?" continued the soldier. "The Land of Goodies?" and before Saucepan Man could reply, the soldiers marched him into the toy fort.

Meanwhile, Joe, Fran and Moonface were walking slowly along admiring all the different toys around them. Fran picked up a strange-looking helmet.

"And what are you?" she wondered.

To her astonishment, the helmet replied. "I'm all your dreams come true. Put me on your head and dream your favourite dream."

Fran put the helmet over her head and gasped with amazement. She was sure she really was at the bottom of the sea! All around her she could see wonderful underwater creatures. A school of dolphins frolicked nearby and Fran felt herself swimming towards them.

"Wheeee! I won!" shrieked Beth arriving back on her skateboard, followed by Silky. "Whatever's Fran doing?"

Fran was standing in the street, still wearing the helmet and making swimming motions with her arms.

"Search me," answered Joe. "Whatever it is, it's certainly keeping her quiet."

At that, Moonface suddenly jumped. "Search you? Search? That reminds me of something. Now what . . . aah! Saucepan Man!"

"Oh no!" cried Beth. "Saucepan Man! I'd almost forgotten!" She ran up to a family of Teddy Bears who were just passing. "Excuse me . . ."

"Sorry," said the largest Teddy. "Can't stop now. Off on rather an important picnic, don't you know!"

Moonface walked up to the bear. "Well, this is quite important, too. You haven't seen a funny little chap wearing lots of noisy clattering saucepans, have you? He clanks rather?"

The Teddy Bears whispered to each other and then the largest one turned to Moonface. "Friend of yours, is he?" he said sternly.

"You've seen him? Where is he?" cried Moonface.

"He's in the Toy Fort over there," said the Teddy, pointing towards it. "He was arrested by the Toy Patrol for stealing!" He turned on his heel and called to the other bears. "Come on, we don't mix with riff-raff!" and he and the other bears marched away.

Joe began to walk towards the fort. Fran was still wearing the helmet and still dreaming.

Beth tapped her on the shoulder. "Come on, Fran."

Together with Moonface and Silky, the three children walked up to the entrance to the fort.

"I don't understand it," said Beth. "Saucepan isn't a thief."

"Well, no," agreed Moonface. "But suppose he thought he was in the Land of Goodies. Everything's free there. You can take whatever you want and no-one minds."

"So he might have gone into the sweet-shop over there . . ." began Beth.

". . . and helped himself," finished Moonface.

Silky was gazing up at the fort. "Look!" she cried.

High above them, peering out through the bars of a turret window, was Saucepan Man.

Fran was back in the real world again, having taken off her helmet. "Poor Saucepan!" she said.

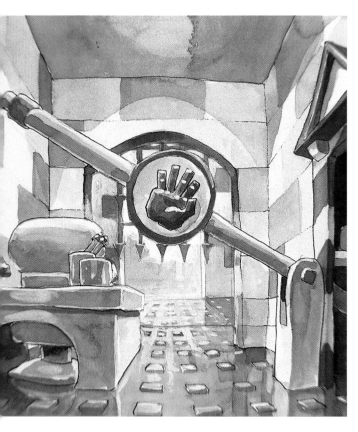

"How are we going to get him out?" asked Beth.

Moonface thought hard. He paced back and forth, back and forth, and walked smack into the window of a fancy dress shop. He gazed at all the costumes. "Aha!" He had an idea.

A few minutes later, Joe came out of the shop, he was wearing the uniform of a toy army officer. In one hand he carried a bag and in the other a large hat. "Are you sure this is going to work?" he asked Moonface, looking worried.

"Er, well, no," said Moonface. "But have you got a better idea?"

Joe pulled on his hat, took a deep breath and marched up to the fort.

"Who goes there?" demanded one of the sentries, stepping towards Joe. "Stand to attention when addressing an officer!" ordered Joe.

The two soldiers quickly stood up straight and saluted.

"That's better," said Joe. "Stand at . . . wait for it, wait for it . . . stand at . . . EASE!"

The two soldiers relaxed, and Joe grinned to himself.

"By the right," he ordered, "on one leg . . . quick . . . HOP!"

The toy soldiers began to hop up and down and as they did so, Joe marched past them into the fort. He quickly made his way up to the turret where Saucepan Man was imprisoned.

Saucepan Man was still peering sadly out of the window when Joe opened his cell door. He turned as Joe walked in, but didn't recognise him in the soldier's uniform.

"Please," Saucepan Man cried. "You've got to let me out. It's all a mirrible hostake!"

"You mean a horrible mistake, Saucepan," said Joe, taking off the hat.

"Joe! How did you get in here?"

"Never mind that," said Joe. "You've got to dress up like me." He opened the bag he was carrying and took out another soldier's uniform. "Put this on. We're going to get you out of here." He began to remove the pots and pans that were hanging from Saucepan Man's body and put them into the bag.

A few minutes later, Joe and Saucepan Man, dressed as soldiers, marched across the parade ground towards the drawbridge. They were almost there when a soldier shouted, "The prisoner has escaped! Sound the alarm!"

The portcullis started to come down. Joe and Saucepan ran towards it. "Hurry, we'll be trapped inside the fort," gasped Joe. They reached the portcullis in the nick of time and threw themselves under it just as one of the pursuing soldiers caught up with them. Angrily, the soldier turned to the two sentries, who were still hopping up and down.

"Stop fooling about you two and get after them!" he ordered, but the two soldiers were so tired after all their hopping, they collapsed in a heap.

Joe and Saucepan Man reached the others just as Beth spotted something behind them.

"Joe, Saucepan Man! Look out!" she shouted.

Three fierce-looking robots were trundling out of the fort, lights flashing. Their robotic voices echoed eerily around.

"Eradicate! Annihilate! Obliterate!" they repeated, as they set off after the friends.

"Help! What do we do now?" groaned Moonface.

"Get back to the tree," urged Beth.

The six friends reached the top of the ladder with the robots close behind.

"Decimate! Castigate! Devastate!" screamed the robots. "Intimidate! Expurgate! Fumigate!"

Moonface was the last to get onto the ladder. "Ha ha! You can't get down here!" he jeered, but he was wrong. The three fierce robots hooked onto the ladder and started to climb down.

"Dessicate! Excruciate! Depredate!"

Beth, Fran, Joe, Silky, Saucepan Man and lastly Moonface piled into Moonface's house and he slammed the door behind him.

"There, that should . . ."

But with a loud crashing, grating sound, the robots began to break down the door. A minute later they were inside Moonface's house.

"Deprecate! Objurate! Relegate!"

Suddenly, there was a shout from the doorway. It was the Angry Pixie.

"Now look here!" he cried. "I've told you lot before! It's come to something when a pixie can't have a little afternoon snooze in peace!"

The robots turned to face him and furiously, he pushed the nearest one in the chest. Surprised, the robot bumped backwards into the one behind him, which tumbled, head over heels, straight down the Slippery Slip. The next robot overbalanced and toppled towards the hole, grabbing the third robot as it fell. With a tremendous clanking and clattering, the three robots shot down the Slippery Slip all the way to the bottom of the tree, and out onto the grass, where they disintegrated into several hundred pieces. A little speaker came to rest beside a bush and a small voice could be heard.

"Oh . . .   botherate!"

Back up at the top of the tree in Moonface's house, the friends were congratulating the Angry Pixie, who was not looking quite as angry as usual.

"Well done. You were brilliant!" laughed Beth.

"Now that's what I call a close thing," said Moonface with a grin.

"You must come to my party!" cried Saucepan Man happily.

Fran held out a bowl of sweets. "Here, have a Toffee Shock," she said.

"Er, I don't think that's such a good idea, Fran," Joe started to say, but the Angry Pixie had already popped it into his mouth. His face started to go red and his cheeks began to bulge. Then he flew up into the air, and zoomed round the room, stars shooting out of his head. Finally, the Toffee Shock exploded and the Angry Pixie landed back on the floor with a bump. He looked furious, his face all red and his fists clenched.

"Oh dear," said Fran. "I didn't . . ."

The Angry Pixie spoke. "That was . . . quite delicious!" and he gave a huge smile. Now Saucepan Man's party could begin at last!

The Land of Dame Tickle

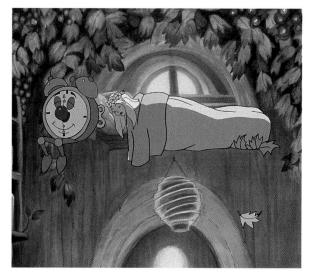

The early morning sun peeped through the leaves of the Faraway Tree and in through the window of Silky's little house, where she was fast asleep in bed. Beside Silky, also fast asleep, was Tock, the wonderful clock that she had found in the Land of Take-What-You-Want. As the hands on Tock's face reached six o'clock, his alarm began to ring.

"What? What's happening?" cried Tock as he awoke. "Where am I? Who's making all that noise?" Then he realised it was his alarm ringing and quickly silenced his bell to stop it waking Silky. He tiptoed outside the house and was standing on a branch when he heard a clanging and a clashing and a clattering.

A moment later Saucepan Man appeared. "Morning Tock. Where are you off to so bright and early?"

Tock smiled at Saucepan Man. "I thought I'd do a spot of exploring," he said and pointed up to the hole in the clouds above their heads.

Saucepan Man was a bit deaf because his pots and pans made such a noise all the time. He looked up at the top of the tree. "Boring?" he said, mishearing Tock. "I shouldn't think so. The lands in the clouds are never boring!"

With an amused smile, Tock set off up the tree and then up the little ladder, closely followed by Saucepan Man.

A few minutes later, Tock climbed through the hole in the clouds into a strange land. He looked around him. He was just thinking how very ordinary it all looked, when a shadow fell over him.

"Well, well, well. A little walking clock, eh?" said a voice and a hand reached out and picked him up.

A moment later Saucepan Man appeared through the hole in the clouds. "Tock? Where have you . . . ?" he started to say, and then he saw Tock struggling to get free. "Hey, put him down! Put him down!" he shouted, running after Tock as he was carried away.

In the Faraway Tree, Silky woke with a start. Someone was knocking loudly on her door.

"Come on! Come on! Open up! I've got a bone to pick with you! Come on! I know you're in there. Open this dooooooooooo . . . or!" As Silky opened the door, the Angry Pixie fell into her house.

"Is something the matter?" asked Silky sleepily.

"I should say there is!" shouted the Angry Pixie. "Your clock!"

"Tock? What about him?" asked Silky.

"Sounding his alarm bell at six o'clock in the morning, that's what! And then Saucepan Man joined him. With all his clatterings, that made matters worse! At least they've gone now. Up through the hole in the clouds and . . ."

But before he could continue, cheerful voices floated up the tree. It was Joe, Fran and Beth.

"Hallo!" cried Fran. "We got up specially early today."

Beth noticed Silky was looking worried. "Silky, is something the matter?" she asked.

Silky turned to her. "Well, I hope not. But it's Tock. He's gone . . ."

The Angry Pixie interrupted her. "BE QUIET all of you. I haven't finished talking!" Everybody turned to the Angry Pixie and silence fell.

"Oh, Budleigh Salterton! You've made me forget what I was going to say!" and with that, the Angry Pixie stamped off, muttering crossly to himself.

Joe turned to Silky. "What were you saying, Silky? Something about Tock?"

"He's gone," replied Silky. "And according to the Angry Pixie, he's gone up through the hole in the clouds with Saucepan Man."

"Well, what are we waiting for?" cried Joe. "Let's go and find them!"

"I'll go and get Moonface," said Fran.

A few minutes later, the three children, together with Silky and Moonface, came through the hole in the clouds, into the unknown land. In the distance they could see a little shop.

"Where are we?" asked Fran.

"I'm not too sure," said Moonface. "But if it's where I think it is, it's a good job I brought my purse!" He took a large purse out of his pocket, shook it loudly and then set off towards the shop. "Come on. We'll ask in that shop over there."

As they drew nearer they could see the shop more clearly.

"What a lovely little shop!" cried Fran. "I bet it sells sweets and chocolates and all sorts of wonderful toys and books and things . . ."

Two cross little pixies came out through the door of the shop. One of them was holding a large gobstopper in his hand.

"See?" said Fran. "I said it would sell sweets!"

The pixies looked at her. "Yeah," said one of them. "Well, I just hope you can afford them. We had to save up for two weeks for this." And he and his friend walked off arguing about who should suck the gobstopper first.

"Save up for two weeks? For a gobstopper?" said Joe, astonished, and he followed the others into the shop.

Inside the shop were jars of sweets, boxes of chocolates, tins of biscuits, cakes and cookies, all looking delicious. Behind the counter stood a large, forbidding woman, called Dame Tickle.

The children stared around them, open-mouthed in wonder at the array of sweets. Moonface stepped

up to the counter and Dame Tickle glared down at him.

"We were wondering . . ." began Moonface.

"Oh, were you? Wondering, eh?" said Dame Tickle.

"Yes," replied Moonface. "Er . . . you haven't by any chance seen a walking clock around these parts? And a chap wearing lots of pots and pans?"

Dame Tickle looked thoughtful. "I might be able to help you. If you were to give me say . . . fifty gold pieces?"

Moonface sighed and opened his purse. He poured a stream of gold coins into Dame Tickle's outstretched hand. She smiled greedily at the money.

"Well?" asked Moonface.

"Well what?" asked Dame Tickle.

Silky was growing impatient. "Have you seen them?" she asked.

Dame Tickle looked annoyed. "No," she said. "Now, unless you want to buy something, be off with you."

The five friends walked slowly along the path outside the shop. After a while, they came to a narrow, winding road that crossed their path. Painted across the road was a zebra crossing. They were just about to walk across when they heard a loud shout.

"Stop!" And from behind a bush appeared Dame Tickle, wearing the uniform of a crossing attendant.

"Don't you know your road drill?" she asked.

"Of course we do," said Fran. "Look right, look left, look right again, then if the road is clear . . ."

". . . you pay me twenty-five gold pieces and walk across," finished Dame Tickle.

"What?" cried everyone together.

"That's the rule," said Dame Tickle.

"Just a minute," said Beth. "Wasn't that you in the shop just now?"

"That information will cost you a hundred gold coins," snapped Dame Tickle.

"You must be joking!" cried Beth.

Things were turning nasty, so Moonface hastily took out his purse and counted out the money.

"There. Twenty-five gold coins. Now can we cross?"

"No," said Dame Tickle. She pointed up the road. "Cars coming." She stepped out into the road and held up her hand. Two tiny cars, driven by two pixies, screeched to a halt.

"Twenty gold pieces?" asked one of them.

"Twenty-five," demanded Dame Tickle. "The rate's gone up since this morning."

Gloomily, the pixies counted out the coins and drove on. Dame Tickle turned to Moonface. "Right, you can cross now . . . after you've paid me twenty-five gold pieces."

"But we already have," cried Moonface.

"I know you have," agreed Dame Tickle. "But that was five minutes ago."

Moonface took out his purse and counted out yet more coins, but he was one coin short.

"Here," he said. "You might as well take this, too." And he handed Dame Tickle the empty purse. He and the others began to cross the road. Dame Tickle stopped them.

"What now?" asked Moonface impatiently.

"Twenty-five gold coins per leg. If you want to walk across, it will be another twenty-five gold coins each."

The friends looked at one another.

"We'll hop, thank you," said Moonface and they all hopped across the road.

Dame Tickle dropped the gold coins into the purse with a satisfied smile.

Moonface, Silky, Joe, Fran and Beth continued along the path looking for Saucepan Man and Tock. Not far away, was a building, and when they got closer they saw several young pixies standing on their heads outside.

"What's going on there?" wondered Fran.

"It looks like the school," said Silky.

"Yes," agreed Fran. "But why are they all standing on their heads?"

"They probably have to pay if they want to use their feet," grinned Joe.

"I'm going to find out," said Fran and she ran on ahead, into the playground and up to one of the pixies.

"Hallo," she said, bending down so she could see the pixie's face. "Why are you all standing on your heads?"

"It's the rules," the pixie whispered to her. "During playtime, we have to stand on our heads and keep perfectly quiet and still, or else . . ."

"Or else? Or else what?" asked Fran.

"The B. P. T. F!"

"B. P. T. F. Um. That spells . . . biptuff? What's a biptuff?"

Before the pixie could answer Fran, a loud bell rang. With sighs of relief the pixies all turned the right way up and marched towards the school door. As Joe, Beth, Silky and Moonface caught up with Fran, they heard a familiar voice.

"Come along, you don't want to be late for lessons, do you?"

"Oh no, not her again," muttered Beth.

Dame Tickle noticed the five strangers. "Ah! New bugs, eh? Well, I'll soon have you licked into shape. And if I don't, it's the B. P. T. F. for the lot of you!"

"There!" said Fran. "She said it too! The biptuff! What is the biptuff?"

"You don't want to know," said Dame Tickle. "Now inside with you before I start to get cross," and she bundled them in through the school door.

Inside the classroom, Moonface, Silky, Joe, Fran and Beth sat at their desks in a row, alongside the pixies.

"Right, out with your books," said Dame Tickle. "And . . . you!" She pointed at a trembling pixie in the front row. "Listen carefully now! Three trains leave the station at the same time. One goes to Timbuktu, one goes to pieces and one goes off the rails. What's the number you first thought of?"

The pixie went pale. "Er, three?" he asked hopefully.

"No, you numbskull!" shouted Dame Tickle. "The Battle of Trafalgar!" She turned to another pixie. "You! Who put the Lam in a-lamma-damma-ding dong? Was it a) King Boffo the third of Guatemala; b) Bertie the Flying Broom Cupboard or c) a box of gerbils?"

The pixie looked blank. "Er . . . I . . . er . . ."

"Quickly! Quickly!" demanded Dame Tickle. Fran by this time had had enough. She got up from the desk and glared at their tormentor.

"This is stupid!" she said. "All these questions are just silly. And so are you! And another thing, where's Silky's clock? And Saucepan Man? There are some sensible questions for you! OK!"

There was a sharp intake of breath from the pixies and Dame Tickle turned a baleful eye in Fran's direction. A heavy silence fell on the school room. What would Dame Tickle do?

"Oh dear, oh dear. I'm going to have to teach you all a lesson. It's time for the B. P. T. F!"

"What is the biptuff?" said Fran.

There was a flash of lightning and a crack of thunder. Dame Tickle reached down to a long painted metal cylinder that stood beside her desk. From inside it she took out . . . The Big Pink Tickling Feather!

The pixies all screamed with fear as Dame Tickle began to lunge to left and right. As the feather touched a pixie or one of the children, they immediately began to laugh hysterically.

Soon the entire classroom was howling with laughter, all but Joe, who had hidden behind his desk. As the rest of the class struggled for breath, giggling and guffawing, chuckling and chortling, Joe crept around the room until he was behind Dame Tickle.

"Right!" he cried. "Let's see how you like a taste of your own medicine!" and he grabbed the feather out of Dame Tickle's hand and began to tickle her.

"Hee hee hee!" giggled Dame Tickle. "Give that ha ha ha back you little hee hee hee worm! You're going to ho ho ho regret this! I'll hee hee hee tear you limb from ha ha ha . . ." and laughing hysterically Dame Tickle staggered backwards into a cupboard. The door flew open and books, papers, chalk, erasers, pencils and pens tumbled out onto the floor, and along with everything else, out fell Tock and Saucepan Man!

"It's Tock!" cried Silky.

"Thank goodness!" cried Saucepan Man. "There's not enough room to swing a kettle in there!"

"Quick! Hee hee!" said Moonface, still laughing hilariously. "Let's get out of ha ha here!"

The three children, Moonface, Silky, Tock and Saucepan Man fled from the room.

"Come back hee hee here!" laughed Dame Tickle. "You haven't paid your school fees hee hee hee yet! Ha ha ha!"

She tried to chase them but, helpless with laughter, fell over a pile of giggling pixies.

As the friends ran towards the hole in the clouds, they couldn't stop laughing. Saucepan Man looked puzzled.

"Have I missed something?" he asked. "Did someone tell a joke?"

Back in Moonface's house later that day, Beth, Fran, Moonface and Silky were still giggling, though not quite as much as before. Joe was trying to explain to Tock and Saucepan Man what had happened.

"So I grabbed her feather and tickled her," he finished.

Moonface laughed. "Ha ha ha! If it hadn't cost me so many gold pieces, hee hee hee, I'd be laughing about the whole affair! Ha ha ha!"

Tock was feeling uncomfortable. He fidgeted about.

"Tock, is something the matter?" asked Silky.

"There seems to be something stuck inside me," said Tock. "It could be anything. That cupboard was so full of . . ." As he spoke, he opened the little door in his back, and pulled out a heavy purse. "Ah! that's better!"

"That's my purse!" cried Moonface in delight. "And look, there's all my money in it!"

"You're welcome to it," said Tock. "It was giving me dreadful indigestion!"

"Thank you!" said Moonface, smiling. "I've really got something to laugh about now!"

"Listen to me, Tock," said Silky, trying to be stern. "You're not to go wandering off on your own again. Next time, you might not be so lucky!"

Beth looked across at Tock. "Wow! Look at the time!"

Tock tried to look at his own face, and failed. "It's no good. I can't. It makes me dizzy," he said.

"I'm sorry," laughed Beth. "I meant that our parents will be wondering where we are."

"Come on! Off we go down the Slippery Slip!" said Fran. "Goodbye Moonface! Goodbye Silky!" With a wave to their friends, the three children climbed into the hole and whizzed down to the foot of the Faraway Tree.

The Land of Ice and Snow

Joe, Fran and Beth were climbing slowly up the branches of the Faraway Tree to visit Moonface.

"I hope he's in," said Beth.

"Where else would he be?" asked Joe.

"He could be anywhere," cried Fran. "He could be in the Land of Make Believe or the Land of Baby Animals or the Land of Lost Toys. I hope he's not in the Land of Goodies because he'll have eaten so much that he won't want any of Joe's homemade banana toffee and . . ."

"Fran . . ." interrupted Beth.

"Yes?" said Fran, stopping for a moment.

"Moonface is right, you know," said Joe laughing. "You could talk *both* hind-legs off a donkey!"

"You two are really cheeky sometimes!" said Fran.

As the three children approached Moonface's door, Silky, the fairy, joined them.

"Ooh, what's in that paper bag, Beth?" she asked. "It smells delicious!"

"It's some toffee we made," explained Beth. "We thought that you and Moonface would like some."

"I'd love some," said Silky. "Let's go and ask Moonface." And she knocked loudly at his door.

Inside, Moonface was dozing on a chair. He leapt up and bumped his head on the shelf above him. An inkwell on the shelf slowly toppled over showering him with ink. Moonface rushed to open the door with ink trickling down his face.

"Oh, it's you! How lovely," he said with a grin.

"What have you been up to?" asked Beth.

Moonface shrugged and laughed. "Little accident with some ink. Come in and I'll get myself cleaned up." He beckoned the others inside, and started wiping his face with his handkerchief.

"Do you like home-made banana toffee, Moonface?" asked Beth.

Moonface beamed at Beth. "Do I like toffee? Do stars have wings? Do the birds twinkle in the sky at night?"

The children stared at him.

"Er . . . no . . ." said Fran, almost speechless for once.

Moonface looked puzzled. "Don't they? Oh - I must have got it wrong. But I do *love* toffee!"

Beth held out the bag. "It's made from Joe's special recipe."

Moonface took a huge lump of toffee and put it into his mouth. "Gwwfkkmmngwmbl!" he said.

"I think he likes it," translated Silky.

"I hope you're right!" said Beth and handed the toffee round to the others.

While they were all busy chewing, they heard a clattering and a clanging outside, and a moment later, Saucepan Man came in.

"Hello, one and all!" he said. "You've got to come up the ladder! It's all beautiful and snowy and . . ."

"Like a land of ice and snow?" asked Joe.

"What do you mean you don't know?" said Saucepan Man, mishearing as usual, as the continuous rattle of his saucepans made him a little deaf. "It's wonderful. Snow in the middle of summer!"

Joe went over to join Saucepan Man. "What are we waiting for then," he said, excitedly. "Let's go!"

"Yes, snow!" said Saucepan Man. "I wish you'd listen." He and Joe hurried out of the door and set off up the tree.

"Gwwwwfkmnnn! Pgghfggmmmmn!" cried Moonface. He and Silky grabbed Fran and Beth before they could follow.

"What's the matter, Moonface?" asked Beth. "Aren't you coming too?"

"Gwwgggfgggllll!" cried Moonface, still struggling to speak through his mouthful of toffee.

"I think he's trying to warn us about something," said Silky.

With a huge effort, Moonface swallowed the toffee and spoke. "Yes! The Land of Ice and Snow!" he gasped. " It's very dangerous! There are polar bears up there - big white bears with big white teeth and big white paws with big white claws!"

Without another word, they rushed out after Joe and Saucepan Man.

"We must catch up with them before they climb up into the clouds," said Beth, nearly crying.

Joe and Saucepan Man were already near the top of the ladder. Faintly, from below, Joe heard voices calling, but he couldn't catch the words because of the clanking of Saucepan Man's pots and pans. He thought the others were trying to catch up and shouted back down the ladder.

"Come on, Slowcoaches! Last one through the clouds is a snowman's . . ." but his words were cut short as he found himself in the midst of a snowstorm. "Oh wow! Look at the snow!"

He pushed on up the ladder and suddenly felt something catch at his shirt collar. It was a large fish hook, which was dangling down through the hole in the clouds. Another hook caught onto Saucepan Man and then he and Joe felt themselves being hauled up through the hole in the clouds . . .

In the Land of Ice and Snow, a pair of large, fierce-looking polar bears were standing by the hole in the clouds, fishing. They started to reel in their catch.

"Ha ha!" said the first. "Caught me a big one here, Igor!"

"Bet it's not as big as mine, Boris," said the other one.

Then they saw Joe and Saucepan Man dangling at the end of their hooks.

"Those aren't fish," said Boris.

"No," agreed Igor. "Better throw them back."

The two huge bears began to disentangle Joe and Saucepan Man from their fish hooks. Boris was just about to throw Saucepan Man back down the hole when Igor stopped him.

"Hold on. I've just had a thought! I bet these two would make a good job of spring-cleaning the igloo!"

"You mean . . . ?"

"I certainly do!" said Boris and he seized Saucepan Man. "I've been wanting to say goodbye to those tiresome household chores for ages."

"No more laundry blues for us," agreed Igor, and he grabbed Joe, who began to struggle.

"What's going on?" cried Joe angrily.

"Oh, sorry," said Igor. "Of course. No-one told you, did they?"

"It's your lucky day, Sunshine," said Boris. "You have just found employment in one of the most sought-after igloos in the district!"

The bears trudged over the snow carrying their two new servants. As they walked, an icy wind blew and the hole in the clouds began to ice over.

Down below, near the top of the tree, Beth and Fran were still following Joe and Saucepan Man.

"Beth! Look!" called Fran. "The hole's getting smaller!"

"It's icing up!" cried Beth.

By the time they reached the top of the ladder, the hole was completely frozen over. Beth banged her fists on the ice, but it was frozen solid . . .

Up in the Land of Ice and Snow, Joe and Saucepan Man were feeling cold and unhappy.

"Where are you taking us?" asked Joe.

A moment later, they arrived at a large igloo. "Here we are," said Igor. "Our igloo!"

"Yes. And you're just in time to start work," added Boris.

"Jerk? Who are you calling a jerk?" said Saucepan Man, bridling.

Boris and Igor just looked at each other.

Inside the igloo was a terrible mess. There were dirty plates, pots and pans, cups and saucers, glasses and mugs everywhere. Papers and magazines lay scattered around.

"When was the last time we did the washing up, Igor?" asked Boris.

"Let's see," wondered Igor. "Must be, oooh, a couple of years?"

"Should take them quite a while then," said Boris.

"Some idea of yours, to come to this land," muttered Joe to Saucepan Man as, a few minutes later, the two of them started to work their way through the mounds of washing up.

Igor's voice cut in. "And when you've finished that . . . you can vacuum the floors . . ."

". . . sort out my fish-head collection . . ." chipped in Boris.

". . . clean the harpoons . . ." continued Igor.

". . . and feed the gerbil," finished Boris.

Joe looked at Saucepan Man, rolled his eyes, and turned back to the dishes.

In Moonface's house the others were trying to work out a rescue plan.

At last, Moonface spoke.

"I know!" he shouted. "The three bears!"

"The three bears who live in the wood?" asked Beth.

"They know the polar bears in the Land of Ice and Snow," explained Moonface. "I'm sure they'll be able to help. Come on!" He grabbed a cushion and shot down the Slippery Slip, followed by the others.

A little while later, the four friends arrived at the house of the three bears, on the far side of the Enchanted Wood.

"Here we are," said Moonface knocking at the door.

Inside the house were Daddy Bear, Mummy Bear and Baby Bear.

"Someone's knocking at my door," said Daddy Bear.

"Someone's knocking at my door," said Mummy Bear.

"Someone's knocking at my door," said Baby Bear, "and if they're not careful, they're going to fizzing break it just like that fizzing Goldilocks broke my fizzing chair!"

"Baby Bear!" said Mummy Bear. "It'll be soap and water for you if you carry on like that! Fizzing indeed!"

As they continued to eat their porridge there was another knock at the door. Daddy Bear put down his spoon and went over to the door to open it.

"Moonface! It's you!"

Moonface explained to the bears all about Joe and Saucepan Man. "So do you think you'll be able to help?" he ended.

"Of course!" said Daddy Bear. "Any friend of Moonface is a friend of ours, right?"

"Yeah," agreed Baby Bear. "Except fizzing Goldilocks!"

"Baby Bear," warned Mummy Bear.

"Do you think you could go there and . . ." began Moonface.

"I can do better than that. We can all go there!" said Daddy Bear.

"All? But how?" asked Beth. "The hole in the clouds is iced over and anyway the Land of Ice and Snow will have moved on by now."

Daddy Bear smiled. "Ah, but they don't call this the Enchanted Wood for nothing, you know.

Now, if we all hold hands . . ."

Baby Bear looked at Fran. "I'm not holding hands with a fizzing girl!" he muttered.

Fran fixed him with a stony stare. "You know something? You are a very bad-mannered bear!"

"You going to do something about it?" growled Baby Bear.

"Try me!" jeered Fran.

Beth tried to make peace. "You don't want to mess with Fran, she's a black belt at origami!" she joked.

Baby Bear realised he had met his match. After a moment's pause, he held out his paw to Fran and they joined the circle. The Bears' cottage began to glow with all the colours of the rainbow, then in a fountain of stars, it disappeared, taking the occupants with it.

In the Land of Ice and Snow, Joe and Saucepan Man were still busy with the housework. Joe finished the vacuuming and turned to the bears, who were sitting watching the television.

"Right," he said. "We've finished the . . ." He stopped suddenly. "Look, Saucepan!" he whispered. "The bears are fast asleep!"

He pointed towards the door. Saucepan Man nodded vigorously, rattling his pots and pans loudly. Joe grabbed them to try and keep them quiet. He put his finger to his lips to show Saucepan Man what he meant and very carefully, they started to tiptoe towards the door. Suddenly, with a loud clatter, Saucepan Man slipped on some ice and with a loud crash fell to the floor.

"Whawhazat? What's going on?" The bears awoke and looked round, to see Joe helping Saucepan Man to his feet.

"It's the servants!" said Igor.

" Ere," said Boris. "You've not finished yet! You haven't cleaned the goldfish tank!"

Joe and Saucepan Man ran for the door and out into the snow. The bears hauled themselves to their feet and lumbered after them.

"Which way?" asked Saucepan Man.

"Out of here!" cried Joe, and the two of them raced across the snow, pursued by the bears.

"It's no use! There's nowhere to hide," gasped Joe in despair.

"Something to ride? Where?" replied Saucepan Man.

"Oh, just come on!" said Joe, and they ran round a large pillar of ice. Ahead of them something was twinkling, and before their eyes, a waterfall of stars reached the ground.

"What's that?" asked Saucepan Man, astonished. "It looks . . . it looks like a little cottage!"

"Oh, Saucepan!" exclaimed Joe. "Come on - maybe we can hide there."

Just at that moment, the door opened and someone came out.

"Hey! It's Moonface," he shouted. "Moonface, however did you get here?"

Behind Moonface were Beth, Fran, Silky and the three bears.

"With the help of the three bears and with a little magic," he laughed.

"We need some magic to escape from the bears," cried Joe. "Look out! They're coming and they'll make you their servants too."

The next moment Igor and Boris pounced on Joe and Saucepan Man.

"Got you!" said Boris holding on to Saucepan Man.

Moonface called loudly, "Unhand those two immediately." The two bears only held on tighter to their captives. All of a sudden, from behind, Daddy Bear stepped forward.

"Afternoon Igor, afternoon Boris."

Igor and Boris recognised their cousins, the three bears.

"Hello, it's Daddy Bear and Mummy too, what a nice surprise!" beamed Boris. "How did you get here?"

"Oh, a few magic words and a lot of wishing," said Daddy Bear. "And now we're here, do you think you could let those two go? Friends of ours, d'you see."

The two bears immediately released the two friends.

"But these are our servants," protested Igor.

"No, they're not," explained Mummy Bear gently. "It's Joe and Saucepan Man and it's time they were home."

Igor and Boris thought about what Mummy Bear had said, looked at each other and both said together, "Oh, all right."

Fran went over to the two bears. "You two are very, very bad bears!" she scolded. "Taking other people and forcing them to be your servants isn't very nice you know, and Joe could've been late for tea!"

Boris and Igor backed away from Fran, who finished speaking and ran into the cottage with the others. A moment later, before the astonished eyes of the two bears, the cottage vanished in a cloud of stars.

Igor rubbed his eyes. "How did they do that?" he wondered.

"Search me," said Boris. "Oh well. Back to the igloo."

"Yes," agreed Igor. "Still, at least we won't have to do any housework for another few years!" And arm in arm the two bears plodded off home.

Back in the Enchanted Wood, the three bears' cottage had landed in exactly the right place, in the middle of its garden. The door opened and out walked Joe, Fran, Beth, Moonface, Silky and Saucepan Man. They waved goodbye to the three bears and thanked them warmly for their help.

"Come and see us any time you are passing," invited Mummy Bear.

The three children left Moonface, Silky and Saucepan Man at the bottom of the Faraway Tree and walked up the winding path towards their cottage.

"By the way," said Joe. "What's for tea? I'm starving."

"Spaghetti Bolognese and apple pie," said Beth.

Fran gave a wicked grin. "With ice-cream!"

Joe turned pale. "Oh no! Not ice-cream!" he said, and then joined in the laughter as they ran back home.

PRINTED IN BELGIUM BY
proost
INTERNATIONAL BOOK PRODUCTION